JOHN CONDON AND MATT HUNT

THE
PIRATES
~ ARE ~
COMING!

nosy crow

Every day, Tom climbed
the hill to watch for pirates.

It had been a long time
since anyone had seen them,
but Tom knew that they would be back.

So he waited . . .
and waited . . .
and waited.
Until at last he saw . . .

THE PIRATES ~ ARE ~ COMING!

For Mandy – JC
For Hayley and Bump – MH

First published 2020 by Nosy Crow Ltd, The Crow's Nest, 14 Baden Place, Crosby Row, London SE1 1YW • www.nosycrow.com
ISBN 978 1 78800 678 1 (HB) • ISBN 978 1 78800 679 8 (PB) • Nosy Crow and associated logos are trademarks and/or registered trademarks
of Nosy Crow Ltd. • Text © John Condon 2020 • Illustrations © Matt Hunt 2020 • The right of John Condon to be identified as the author
and Matt Hunt to be identified as the illustrator of this work has been asserted. • All rights reserved. • This book is sold subject to the
condition that it shall not, by way of trade or otherwise, be lent, hired out or otherwise circulated in any form of binding or cover
other than that in which it is published. • No part of this publication may be reproduced, stored in a retrieval system, or transmitted
in any form or by any means (electronic, mechanical, photocopying, recording or otherwise) without the prior written permission of
Nosy Crow Ltd. • A CIP catalogue record for this book is available from the British Library. • Papers used by Nosy Crow are made from
wood grown in sustainable forests. • Printed in China • 10 9 8 7 6 5 4 3 2 1 (HB) • 10 9 8 7 6 5 4 3 2 1 (PB)

. . . a ship!

And quick as a flash, everybody hid.

They waited . . .   and waited . . .

and waited,   UNTIL . . .

. . . it was clear there were NO pirates, just a little fishing boat bobbing home.

"Tom," said the villagers. "That's not even a ship."

"Never mind, Tom," said his dad. "Just remember, pirate ships are BIG."

Tom knew it was very important to keep watching, and so the next day, he went back up the hill.

And again he waited . . .

and waited . . .

and waited.

Until at last he saw . . .

a ship!

A **big** ship.

And once again, everybody hid.

They waited . . .

and waited . . .

and waited,

UNTIL . . .

. . . it was very clear there were STILL NO pirates, just a rusty old steamboat chugging back to shore.

"Tom," said the villagers. "That's the slowest ship we've ever seen!"

"Never mind, Tom," said his dad. "Just remember, pirate ships are big and fast."

Tom knew someone had to keep watching, and so the next day, he went back up the hill. And again he waited . . .

and waited . . .

and waited.

Until at last he saw . . .

a ship! A big ship.

A big, fast ship.

DING!

DING!

"PIRATES!"

shouted Tom.

"THE PIRATES ARE COMING! THE PIRATES ARE COMING! QUICK! EVERYBODY HIDE!"

And once again (but not quite as quickly this time), everybody hid.

They waited . . . and waited . . . and waited, UNTIL . . .

... it was very clear there were DEFINITELY NO pirates, just a big merchant ship sailing into the dock.

"TOM!" said the villagers.
"That is NOT a pirate ship!"

"Never mind, Tom," said his dad gently. "Just remember, pirate ships are big and fast and they have a special pirate flag."

When Tom slowly trudged up the hill the next day, he took with him his favourite book, some crayons and his teddy, and got ready for a long wait.

But suddenly . . .

he saw a ship.

A **big** ship.

A **big**, **fast** ship.

A BIG, FAST ship with a SPECIAL PIRATE FLAG!

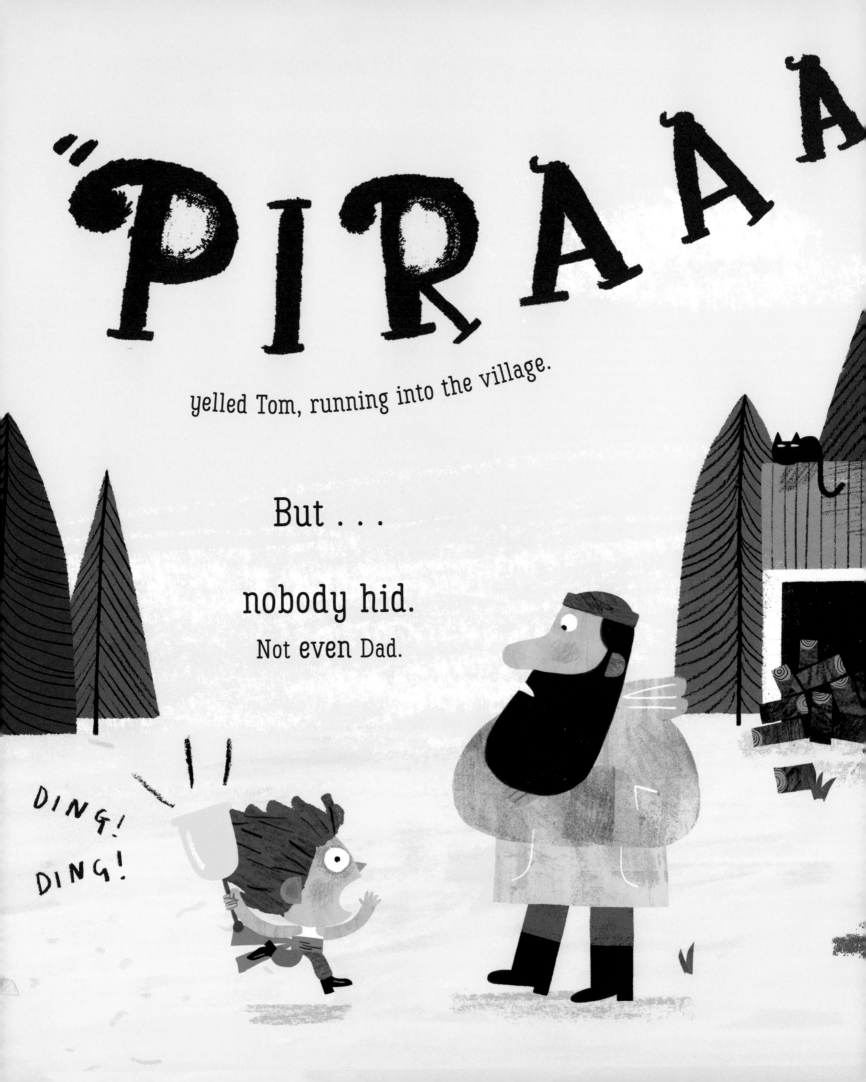

"PIRAAA

yelled Tom, running into the village.

But . . .

nobody hid.

Not even Dad.

DING!
DING!

Meanwhile, the pirate ship sailed silently into the harbour. The gangplank fell with a THUD! And the pirate captain ran ashore, with the pirate crew close behind.

Nobody heard the pirates as they climbed the steps to the village. Nobody heard them as they made their way down the narrow streets. Until . . . .

"SQUAWK!"

cried the captain's parrot.

"The pirates **are** coming!" gasped the villagers.

And this time – just in time – everybody hid . . .

Moments later, the pirates marched into the square.

"Where is everybody?" growled the pirate captain . . .

Then
suddenly . . .

"I missed you, Son!"
said the pirate captain.

"I missed you
more!" said Tom . . .

. . . . "Welcome home, Mum!"